Everything About Easter Rabbits

by Wiltrud Roser
translated by Eva L. Mayer

Thomas Y. Crowell · New York
Harper & Row Junior Books Group

Library of Congress Cataloging in Publication Data
Roser, Wiltrud.
    Everything about Easter rabbits.
    SUMMARY: Describes the special duties of the Easter
Rabbit and how he is distinguished from the ordinary
rabbit which he strongly resembles.
    Translation of Alles über Osterhasen.
    [1. Rabbits—Stories. 2. Easter stories]
I. Title.
PZ10.3.R725Ev   [E]   72-7430
ISBN 0-690-27156-5
ISBN 0-690-27157-3 (lib. bdg.)
ISBN 0-06-443038-3 (pbk.)

Thomas Y. Crowell
Harper & Row Junior Books Group
A Harper Trophy Picture Book
Translation copyright © 1972 by
Thomas Y. Crowell Company, Inc.
Illustrations and German text copyright © 1968
by Atlantis Verlag. Originally published under
the title Alles über Osterhasen.
Published simultaneously in
Canada by Fitzhenry & Whiteside Limited, Toronto.
Designed by Jane Breskin Zalben
Manufactured in the United States of America

First published by Thomas Y. Crowell in 1972.
First Harper Trophy edition, 1983.

Everything About Easter Rabbits

On Easter Sunday the Easter Rabbit comes, as everyone knows.
Some people say that the Easter Rabbit can lay eggs.
Others say that the Easter Rabbit buys eggs from the chickens and
then colors them.
And some will tell you that the Easter Rabbit can neither lay eggs nor
color them. They say he buys the eggs in the Easter Rabbit
department store. Who is right?

All of them.
There are many different kinds of Easter Rabbits.
This book will tell you how to recognize them and what
each one does.

1.

The Genuine, Original Easter Rabbit

Genuine, Original Easter Rabbit   Ordinary Bunny Rabbit

The Genuine, Original Easter Rabbit looks and behaves
just like an ordinary bunny rabbit. He even lives just like
his friends, the ordinary bunny rabbits.

From morning to night he plays games with them, such as Hide-and-Seek and Steal-the-Farmer's-Cabbages.

Three ordinary bunny rabbits look for the G.O. Easter Rabbit who is hiding.

When they race, the G.O. Easter Rabbit always wins.

The Genuine, Original Easter Rabbit always sits upright while he is eating.

But once a year he doesn't have
a minute to spare for games.
That is on **Easter Sunday.**

Then the Genuine, Original Easter Rabbit gets up
at sunrise. He hops through the woods and the meadows
and into the gardens, hiding his many red, blue,
green, yellow, orange, and purple Easter eggs.
He lays the eggs in the soft moss and the high grass.
Best of all he likes to put them in the hazelnut bushes.

He lays his eggs for the poor

and the rich,

for the young and the old,

for the gentle

and the rough,

for the messy and the neat.

Beware!

Never, never try to catch the Genuine, Original Easter Rabbit or the same thing may happen to you that happened to the naughty sons of Farmer Littletwist.

Early one Easter morning the two boys hid under a hazelnut bush. The G.O. Easter Rabbit came along and the two boys quickly covered him with a big laundry basket they had brought along. The bad boys hoped that the Easter Rabbit would leave all his eggs under the basket. Then they would be in the Easter egg business. And the Easter Rabbit actually did leave all the eggs for that village under the basket.

The boys gathered them up quickly and went to stand in front of the village church. There they sold all the eggs to the good people of the village. But no sooner were the boys' pockets full of money and the basket empty than the first eggs came flying back, right smack at their heads. Then all the rest of the Genuine, Original Easter Rabbit's eggs came flying out of all the windows and doors straight at the boys. Hundreds of broken eggs stuck to them and their clothing. It is said that to this day the bad boys still smell of rotten eggs.

Here is a sure way to tell the Genuine, Original Easter Rabbit from an ordinary bunny rabbit:

Walk through the woods with an intelligent dog. If a bunny rabbit hops across your path and the dog treats it like thin air, then you can be sure it is the Genuine, Original Easter Rabbit.

For unlike ordinary bunny rabbits, the Genuine, Original Easter Rabbit has no scent.

2.

The Hardworking Easter Rabbits

There are many of these Easter Rabbits.
The Hardworking Easter Rabbits wear clothes.
They are easy to recognize.

at home, most Hardworking Easter Rabbits wear aprons.

They cannot lay eggs, no matter how hard they try.
Instead, they buy chicken eggs and paint them pretty colors.

Painting eggs is a great art,
but getting the eggs is just as difficult.

The rooster is never glad to see a Hardworking Easter Rabbit
come, begging for eggs. The hens are employed by the farmer
and every egg has to be accounted for by the rooster, who is
in charge.

The Hardworking Easter Rabbit has better luck with those hens
who hide their eggs in the straw or in the field. But even
they are not too happy to give their eggs away.

One must be very polite....

Some pretty hens are glad
to get little presents,

and others enjoy a
long, friendly chat.

Then there is a kind old mother hen who lives with one of the
Easter Rabbit families all year round. Her job is to watch
over the smallest Easter Rabbits and to lay one egg each day.

One week before Easter, egg coloring begins at the homes of the Hardworking Easter Rabbits.
The Hardworking mother Easter Rabbits make all the colors by cooking such things as spinach, onions, coffee grounds, and red beets.
Sometimes the children help.
Hundreds of eggs are being painted by this Hardworking father Easter Rabbit and the children.
The Hardworking grandma Easter Rabbit has colored only three, but they are the prettiest ones of all.

Every Easter Rabbit family has its own pattern and one egg from each family hangs on the Hardworking Easter Rabbits' special Easter tree. Only the young Easter Rabbit children paint alike.
They dip the eggs into the pots of paint, first the top, then the bottom. This makes colorful rings on the eggs.

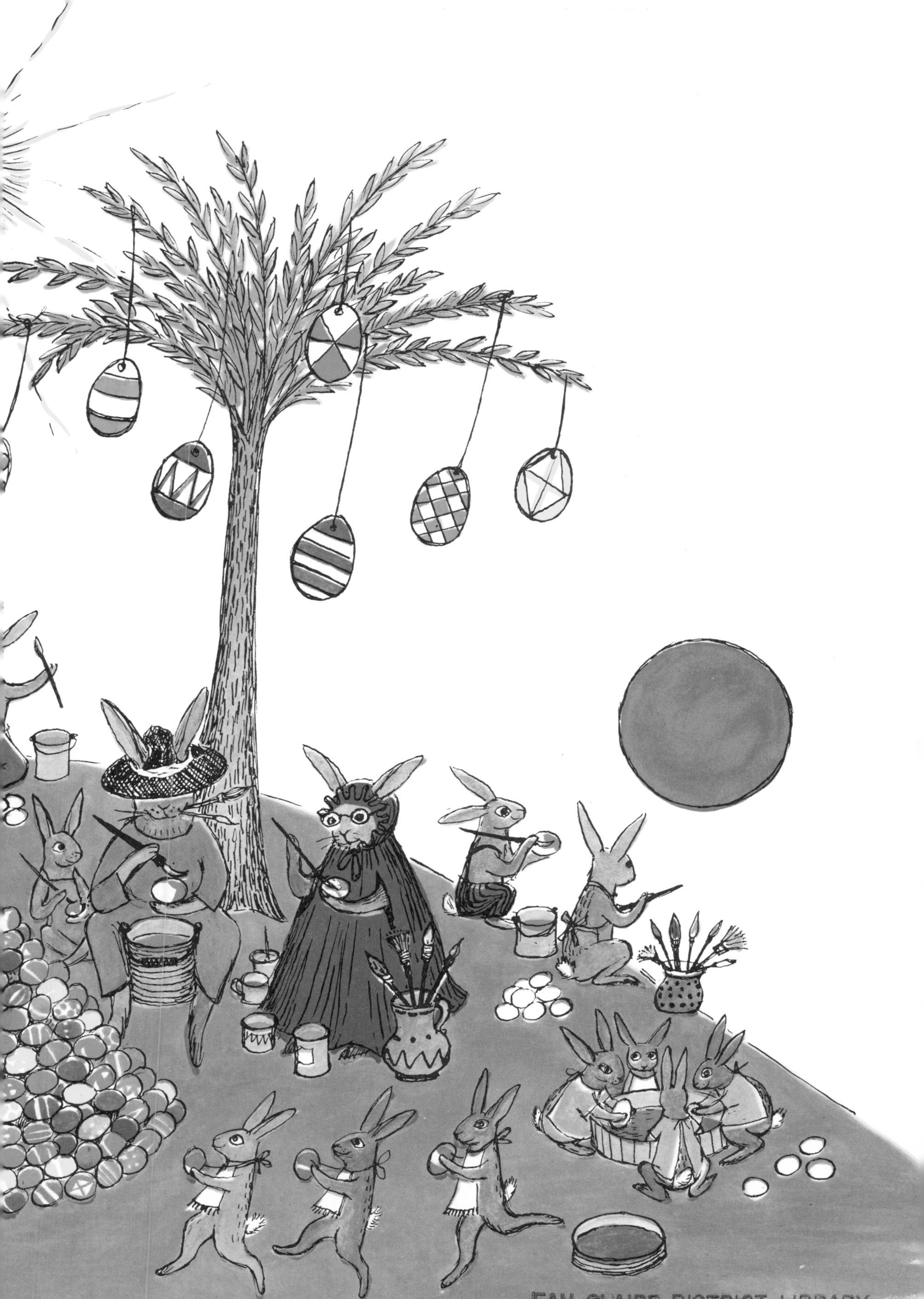

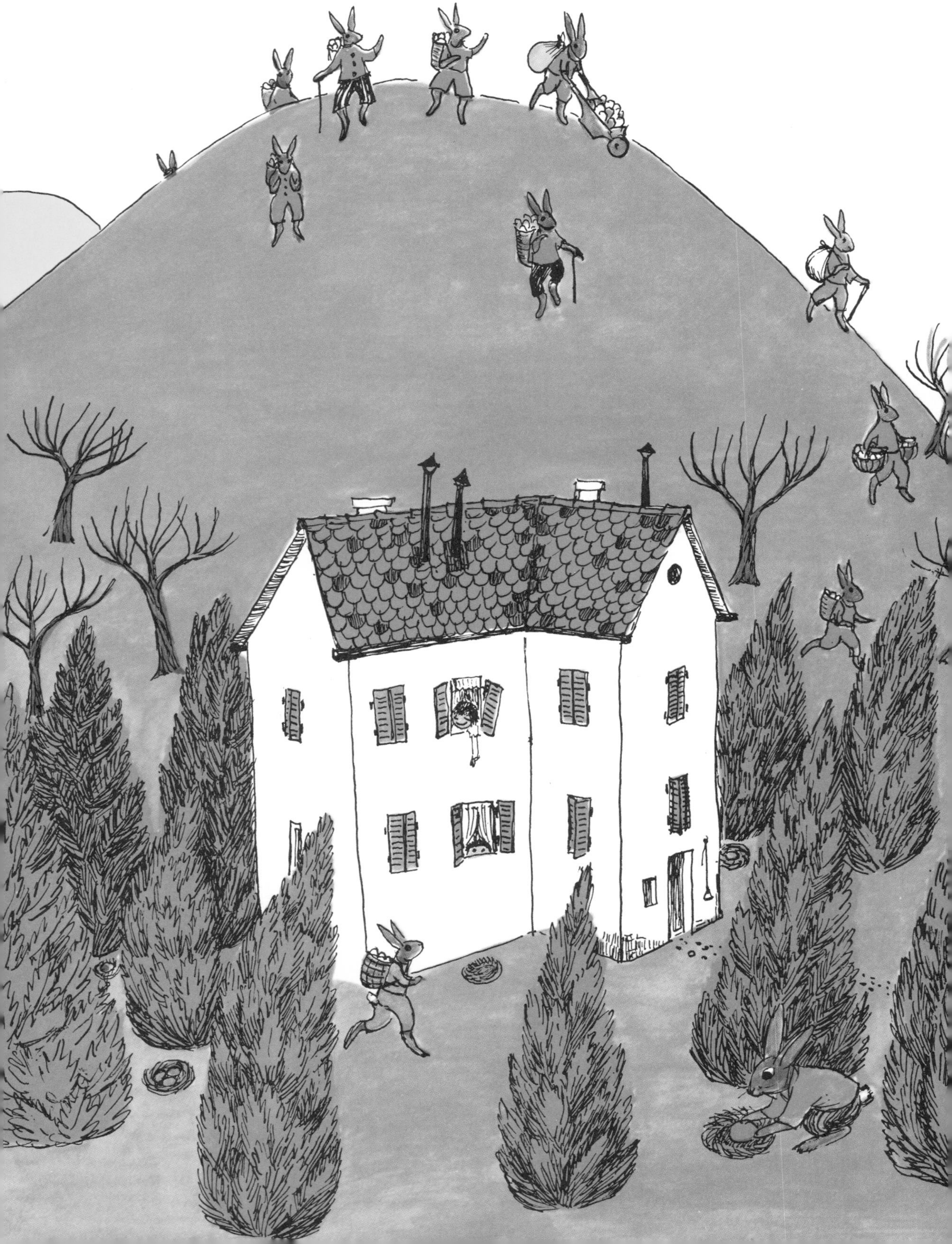

On Easter Sunday the Hardworking Easter Rabbits go forth
in all directions looking for the good children.
Those people who want to please the Easter Rabbits build cozy nests
for them to leave the eggs in.
When an Easter Rabbit sees naughty children, he hops past them
quickly and takes care not to drop even one of his nice eggs.

Every ordinary bunny rabbit can become a Hardworking Easter Rabbit . . .
if he is clever;
if he goes to school on time every morning and is neatly dressed;
if he can sit still and listen attentively to the teacher.

Rabbit Max came without clothes and was sent home by the teacher.

Rabbit Fred listens but he can't sit still.

Rabbit Hilda sits still but she can't listen.

Rabbit Philip can't sit still or listen.

Though they don't like it, these bunny rabbits have to do homework, too.
They have problems like this, for instance:

Arithmetic: 5 children live in one house. 3 are well behaved and 2 are naughty. How many eggs should the Easter Rabbit leave?

Nature Study: Pick a basket of spinach and bring it to school to prepare color for the eggs. (That is especially difficult for little bunny rabbits who can hardly resist eating it right away.)

Art: Draw a picture of your parents.

Some little bunny rabbits do their homework until late at night. Their parents watch over them, but they are not allowed to help them with their homework.

Their young brothers and sisters have long
since gone to sleep in their beds of grass.

Once a bunny rabbit has learned to read and write and to color
an egg beautifully, then he becomes Easter Rabbit King for a day
and is congratulated by everyone.

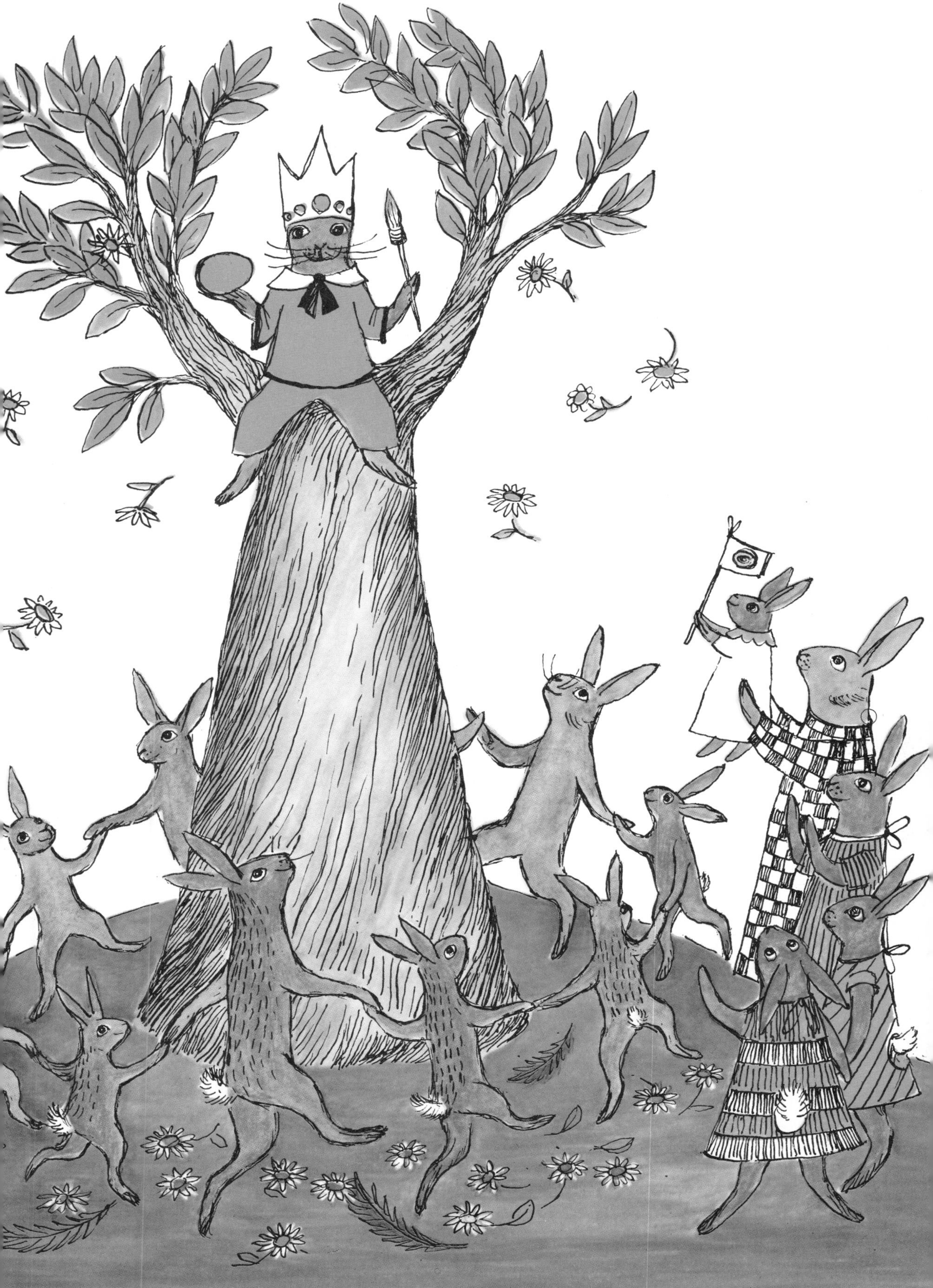

3.

The World-Traveling Easter Rabbit

The World-traveling Easter Rabbit carries a special Easter suitcase.
He cannot lay eggs and has no time for coloring.

He goes to the large Easter Rabbit department store.
There he fills his suitcase with candy eggs, chocolate bunnies,
jelly beans, crayons, balls, pinwheels, kites, picture books
and everything else that strikes his fancy.

Then he zooms away on his motorcycle to give these presents
to good children in the nearest village.

For longer trips, he drives in his red car.

He usually takes the Easter Rabbit Steamboat to go to New York City.

To go to the North Pole, he uses a helicopter.
When the World-traveling Easter Rabbit arrives, the polar bears are
just as happy as the Eskimo children. That is because he often
drops them a toy or two out of his suitcase.

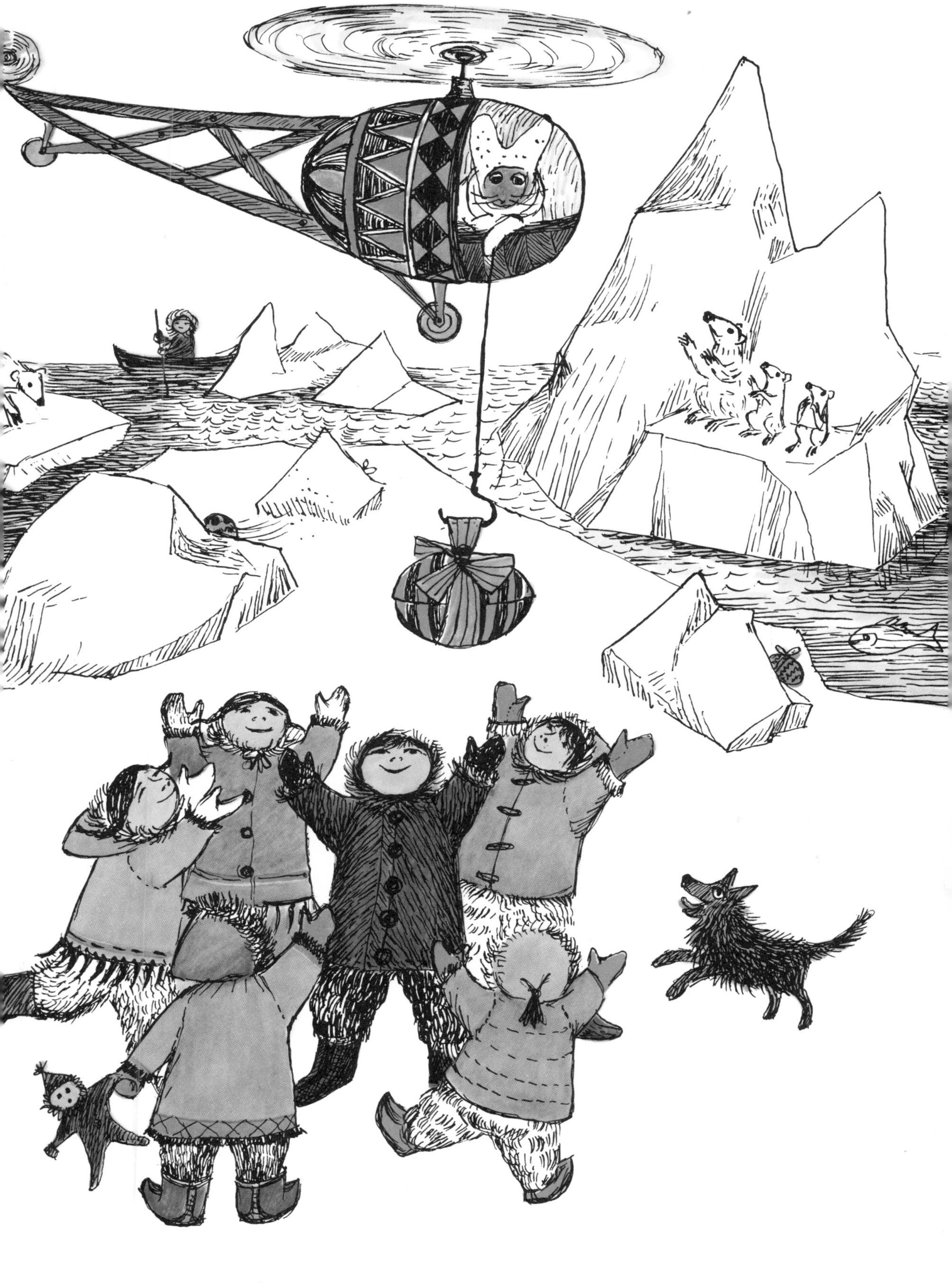

And now you know everything about Easter Rabbits.
Watch carefully to see which one comes to your house.